This book belongs to

For all the children at Treewise
C.F.

First published in 2008 in Great Britain by
Gullane Children's Books
185 Fleet Street, London, EC4A 2HS
www.gullanebooks.com

1 3 5 7 9 10 8 6 4 2

A CIP record for this title is available from the British Library.

ISBN: 978-1-86233-662-9 (hardback edition)
ISBN: 978-1-86233-746-6 (paperback edition)

Printed and bound in Indonesia

This is the Way

by Charles Fuge

This is the way the elephant walks

And this is the way the dinosaur stalks

SNARL
HISS
GNASH!

This is the way the house mouse scurries

SKITTLE
SKATTLE
SKUTTLE!

And this is the way the ladybird hurries

BEETLE
BATTLE
BUTTLE!

This is the way the anteater creeps

PROD
SNUFFLE
POKE!

And this is the way the treefrog leaps

GULP
RIBBIT
CROAK!

This is the way
the orangutan swings

OOH
OOH
OOH!

And this is the way
the tawny owl sings

TAWIT
TAWIT
TAWOO!

This is the way
the bumble bee flies

Bzzz
Bzzz
Bzzz!

And these are my dreams when I close my eyes

ZZZZ ZZZZ ZZZZ!

B
C

Other books by Charles Fuge

My Dad!

What Can a Baby Do?
written by Sarah Churchill

Yip! Snap! Yap!

I Know a Rhino